# THE ADVENTURES OF MELVIN RICHARDSON

## Soul Searching

### W Priggs

*Proof readers: Glowegal Proofers & Part-Time Roofers*
*David J Miller, Missing Word Filler*

# CONTENTS

## PREVIOUSLY, IN THE ADVENTURES OF MELVIN RICHARDSON...

Melvin Richardson died!

The end? Not likely!

Melvin has the chance to appeal his death with the help of the dodgiest lawyer this side of life!

The so-called lawyer, Mr Fitzwilliam, or is it Fitzpatrick, has flamingo legs and a packet of cheese and union crisps, or is it onion?

There's a tiny man with a huge clipboard, a cleaner who cannot speak due to Judge Ice Cream's cat that bit his tongue.. oh, and the cat turns into a walking-frame... and there's a robed librarian in charge of the collected souls in the Grand Soul Library.

Melvin's soul is gone! Not just missing but sold to the People of Pluto's Posterior. Except it didn't go with the batch of ten, having dropped out of the pre-paid consignment.

Close escapes. Lies. Bad writing. It all happens!

Needless to say, Melvin Richardson (the poo that holds his body and soul to-gether) gets back his soul and his body which is still on Earth.

Unfortunately, his body is still under the Mediterranean Sea! And so, Melvin Richardson dies... again...

## AND NOW...

# The Blabbermouth And The Bum

"What about this for a riddle;" a high-pitched voice echoed around the walls of the sceptic tank, which was half-full of gunge (a pink goo with a pair of eyes and a mouth), "tired of laying on my side, my belt too tight to breathe. I'll stand up straight as a stick, twelve others underneath…"

"Noooo." A mouth beside the one with the high-pitched tone appeared next to it in the gunge, a new pair of eyes blinking into view.

"What do you mean no?" The high-pitched voice squealed. "I haven't finished yet! I can never finish…"

"Noooo." The deep voice droned.

"Ohhhh you're so negative! You'd never be the boss of people! Imagine having twelve people underneath *you*, you negative one!"

"You go on foreverrrrrrrr." The deep monotone voice replied.

"You calling me a blabbermouth?!" The high-pitched blabbermouth squealed.

"The answerrrrr to yourrrr riddle," the deep voice corrected, "foreverrrr is infinnnniteeee."

"Depends on your point of view," the high-pitched voice retorted nonchalantly, "and besides, we've moved on from that, the proof's all wrong!"

"In the puddinnnng." The eyes above the droning voice rolled around.

"In the pudding now, is it?" The high-pitched voice rasped. "It was in finny tea earlier, you stupid haddock!"

Suddenly a black sphere landed between the talking mouths and splashed some of the gunge by their eyes. On top of the sphere was some kind of protruding small rope which was burning at one end.

"Do you mind," the high-pitched voice seemed put about, "we're having a private conversation!"

The rope was burning itself smaller.

"Is he shushing me?" The high-pitched voice asked his monotone friend.

"Bommmmb!" The deep voice tried its best to be alarming, but came across just as monotone as before.

"Bum?" The high-pitched voice snapped. "I'm sorry, I re-fuse to talk to a bum!"

The thin rope was burning shorter.

"Bommmmmmmmmb!" The deep voice repeated as its eyes closed, disappearing into the gunge.

"Ohhhh," the high-pitched voice suddenly realised, "bomb. Speak clearer! I thought you said bu…"

The high-pitched voice was cut short by a huge explosion that emanated from the bomb beside it.

The explosion ripped the sceptic tank apart which blew a hole in the outer hull of the transport that was carrying it. Buckling the already weird looking craft, it was sent on a rightward trajectory until the gravity well of a nearby moon slowed it to a stop once more. It was Benny Fitzwilliam's transport. And it was crippled in space.

In the cockpit of a nearby vessel a shadowy figure watched the explosion through the front window. A growl spilled from the shadow's lips, which became laughter as a torpedo was aimed at what remained of Benny Fitzwilliam's transport.

A gloved hand flicked a switch on the controls which made a crackling sound as a megaphone whistled into life. The speaker was on. The shadow's laughter had gone; all that remained was rage.

"Surrender Benny Fitzwilliam to me," a deep voice gnarled into the microphone, "or prepare to die!"

Suddenly a dollop of pink gunge landed on the windscreen. It had a pair of eyes and a mouth that smiled when it saw the creature within the cockpit. It was some kind of thick liquid that Benny Fitzwilliam's transport had been carrying.

The shadow growled. Flicking on the windscreen wipers to remove the weird entity outside, it only managed to create a greater smear with a wider smile.

"Comply or die!" The shadow growled into the microphone, ignoring the gunge on the windscreen. It was suddenly more impressed with the rhyme it had accidentally conjured and tried to do another one. "Surrender or your life will ender!"

Across space, Benny Fitzwilliam's transport was in trouble. The explosion of the sceptic tank had caused violent turbulence throughout, knocking everyone onboard to the floor.

"What was that?" The tiny man removed the rubble that covered him and picked up his clipboard as he stood on shaking legs.

"It's them." Benny Fitzwilliam was on his back under a pile of debris. Something had exploded onboard, and Mr Fitzwilliam knew what that meant; the Marzipans were here!

"It's the sceptic tank that exploded!" the tiny man glared through the huge window before him, watching the remnants of what used to be the tank floating away.

"It's the Marzipans." Benny Fitzwilliam spoke like he was already dead.

"Why aren't they telling us what they want?" The tiny man replied hastily.

"They are," Benny Fitzwilliam breathed his response, "they just don't know that sound doesn't travel through space."

"Concede or bleed!" The shadowy figure on the Marzipan vessel wasn't yelling into the microphone anymore, but almost singing out the rhymes.

"Submit, you…" Feedback from the speakers whistled through the cockpit and stopped the Marzipan mid-sentence. It didn't matter. The huge megaphone glued to the top of the vessel gave no hint of sound through the emptiness of space. No one onboard Benny Fitzwilliam's transport could hear the mad Marzipan anyway!

"So, how do we know what they want?" The tiny man helped Benny Fitzwilliam onto his flamingo legs.

"It's why the Marzipans are mad; they never get what they want," Mr Fitzwilliam caught his breath, "because they don't realise that no one can hear them!"

"Time's up." The shadowy figure in the cockpit of the Marzipan vessel had finished with the silly rhymes and pressed the torpedo-release button.

"I think they want us dead." The tiny man was now stood at the window at the front of Benny Fitzwilliam's transport, looking into the blackness of space outside.

"It's probably a safe bet." Mr Fitzwilliam replied. He knew what they wanted.

"Well yes, seeing as there's a torpedo heading straight for us." The tiny man pointed his huge clipboard towards the pane of glass beside him.

Mr Fitzwilliam squinted beyond the tiny man. He could see the Marzipan vessel in the cold distance outside and, sure enough, the torpedo it had released that was heading straight for them.

## Six Hours And Sixteen Minutes Before...

"You are not selling my soul!" It hadn't taken Melvin Richardson long to come to his senses as he stood in reception looking at the so-called lawyer and the tiny man with his huge clipboard. He remembered the farce he had endured before, the story of his 'life' and the appeal that had meant nothing, and its purpose to distract him from the fact they were just thieves trying to sell his soul for some vast amount of money!

"The thought never crossed our minds, Mr Richardson!" Mr Fitzwilliam held up his hands in defensive posture, his briefcase dangling by his side.

The tiny man imitated the action, his clipboard held tightly.

"So, you weren't going to pretend to be a lawyer again while my soul is sold?" Melvin spoke through a burrowing frown as he walked towards the pair of idiots.

"Of course not," Mr Fitzwilliam shook his head, "what makes you say that?"

As Melvin reached the pair, he snatched the huge clipboard from the tiny man's hands and read out the bold words he had seen from across the room.

"Things to do today: pretend to be a lawyer, sell Mr Richardson's soul!" Melvin turned the clipboard so they could both read it.

"Well, it's not *my* clipboard," Mr Fitzwilliam looked down at the tiny man beside him and shook his head as if to signify his shame.

Melvin quickly turned the clipboard to read the next few words. "Signed, Benny Fitzwilliam."

"Oh, that." Mr Fitzwilliam looked back at Melvin.

"Who signs a 'to-do' list, anyway?" Melvin was shocked at the stupidity of the pair before him.

"That was yesterday's 'to-do' list!" The tiny man snatched back his clipboard and held it even tighter.

"And I guess your case has a bag of crisps in it so Judge Ice Lolly's cat doesn't bite off our tongues." Melvin looked at the briefcase in the so-called lawyer's hand, remembering what happened to him last time.

"And a banana." Mr Fitzwilliam replied with a smile.

Melvin shook his head. He didn't want to get bogged down in nonsense like before. All he wanted was his life back.

"You're not selling my soul." Melvin repeated in a calm manner; he thought it sounded more menacing that way.

"Wouldn't dream of it, Mr Richardson." Mr Fitzwilliam smiled.

"Good," Melvin shoved past the pair and walked into the corridor, "then take me to it now! And after that you can move my body on Earth. It's still underwater!"

"Oh, so that's why you're back so soon." The so-called lawyer followed on his flamingo legs, the tiny man struggling to keep up the pace behind them.

Melvin stopped and turned to face them. "Don't you know? Surely you have the story of my life to show me?" He spoke in his most sarcastic voice. "Or are those guardian angels playing cards again?"

Mr Fitzwilliam and the tiny man glanced at each other in silence.

"We had to tell you something," Mr Fitzwilliam spoke sincerely, "the human brain is very delicate. If you knew the truth your bum would explode!"

"I'm not interested in your truth," Melvin ignored the so-called lawyer, "I just need you to move my body out of the sea so that when I get back in it I don't drown... again!"

"Well, err..." The tiny man began.

"My soul!" Melvin interrupted, still not interested in what either had to say. "Where is it?"

"It'll be in the Grand Soul Library." Mr Fitzwilliam replied.

"Like it was last time?" Melvin didn't believe him and made it clear in his tone.

"It should still be there now," Mr Fitzwilliam was adamant, "it's where they all go, first of all, to be processed."

"Then let's get a move on." Melvin glared at the so-called lawyer. He didn't know which direction to go and needed him to take the lead.

Mr Fitzwilliam understood and walked on in front, his briefcase swinging merrily by his side.

The double doors of the Grand Soul Library flew open and Melvin pushed his way inside first. The robed librarian was upon him immediately, but soon backed away when he saw Mr Fitzwilliam and the tiny man behind him.

"My soul!" Melvin tried to keep his internal rage at bay. "Where is it?"

"Your soul?" The robed librarian tried to make out he didn't know where it was. "Is that one of the Rs?"

"It's okay," Mr Fitzwilliam smiled, "the cat's out of the bag."

The robed librarian gasped.

"No, no," the tiny man soothed his fears, "not that cat. She's with Judge Ice Cream."

Melvin bowed his head to try and see beneath the black robe of the librarian. It was no use. He couldn't see the face. Melvin remembered pulling back the hood to reveal there was nothing underneath it on their previous encounter, but there had to be someone beneath the cloth. Hadn't there?

Suddenly the cleaner walked into view from one of the dark passageways of the library. He was carrying a briefcase like Mr Fitzwilliam's and smiled as he saw the small crowd gathered by the double doors.

"Got the soul?" Mr Fitzwilliam called out to the cleaner.

The cleaner walked to a small desk beside them, placing the briefcase upon it. He took a piece of paper and a pen in order to scribble his reply (ever since Judge Ice Cream's cat had got his tongue the cleaner had been unable to speak).

'The sole is in the breef kase.' The cleaner held up the first piece of paper for them all to read.

"Excellent," Mr Fitzwilliam beamed, "you see, Mr Richardson. Your soul is here. Panic over."

"Wait a minute," Melvin was having none of it, "how do I know that? You've lied to me before." He was looking at the so-called lawyer.

"Okay," Mr Fitzwilliam was trying not to take offence, "show him."

The cleaner frowned, glancing at the briefcase. He took a pad and pen once more and scribbled out his next etchings; 'R U shure U wont me 2 open it?'

"Open the case man!" Mr Fitzwilliam declared. "Your spelling gets worse! I'm pretty sure you could spell the word 'soul' last time!" He then turned to Melvin. "You know, even with your soul it's no use if your body is under water."

"You can move my body." Melvin had his eyes focused on the briefcase as the cleaner unclasped both locks, before looking towards the flamingo-legged man once more.

"And how do you think we can move your body?" Mr Fitzwilliam asked.

"You caught my soul in a big net," Melvin replied, "I assume that means we're in space somewhere near Earth. If you can catch souls you can move bodies!"

Mr Fitzwilliam's eyes opened wide with surprise. "I think you assume too much."

Melvin turned to glare at the briefcase on the desk once more. The so-called lawyer was lying to him again, he knew. He was probably trying to distract him so that the cleaner wouldn't open the briefcase. Was his soul even in there?

"Open it!" Melvin yelled at the reticent cleaner.

Mr Fitzwilliam nodded his head with silent approval. Shrugging his shoulders, the cleaner flipped open the briefcase.

A white light emanated from the open briefcase. Melvin squinted at it. He could see something else within the briefcase; a spherical object with a protruding unlit fuse.

"Is that a bomb?" Melvin asked with a deep frown.

Suddenly a scream filled the air. Everyone jumped back. The cleaner jumped under the table.

The white light inside the briefcase floated into the air before turning into a ghostly-white apparition. Its eyes like tennis balls. Its teeth like needles. Its scream like ice.

Melvin watched as the robed librarian pulled back his own hood revealing nothing underneath it. The empty black cloth fell silently to the floor. A good way of escaping situations, figured Melvin, and suddenly wished he was nothing but an empty robe!

"There you go," Mr Fitzwilliam spoke as he backed away from the horrific entity floating before them, "what more proof do you need?" He was trying to bluff Melvin into believing the entity before them was *his* soul. After all, their legs all looked the same!

Melvin was backing away too. "Proof? Proof of what? That's not my soul!"

"Are you sure?" Mr Fitzwilliam replied. "Look at the legs!"

"I'm looking at the bomb," Melvin snapped, "what was the plan; to blow up my soul?"

"That's not your soul." Mr Fitzwilliam replied hastily, before realising what he had just said. "Oops."

The entity turned to face the trio, all backing away in fear. It didn't see the reticent cleaner under the table beneath it. It wasn't interested in the empty robe on the floor. A smile grew over its face, beaming wider to show its needle teeth. It was the smile of pure rage, and allowed itself another high-pitched scream to release the anger within.

"You've already sold my soul, haven't you?" Melvin spoke whilst backing away from the ghoulish creature before him.

"We haven't sold your soul." The so-called lawyer spoke through fear, deciding the truth might not be such a bad idea right now.

"Then where is it?" Melvin wasn't convinced.

"We released it," the reply was swift, "into space to see where it goes."

Before Melvin had a chance to reply the ghostly entity swooped down upon him.

The trio dived onto the wooden floorboards as the apparition flew by. Melvin wasn't going to stay. He recognised the ghoulish creature as the one he had released before. It was the one that didn't belong to any alphabetical system that the Grand Soul Library stored souls in. This was one of the souls of the miscellaneous.

Hearing screams behind him, Melvin was quickly on his feet and running to the double doors and freedom. Let the ghoul prey on the so-called lawyer and the tiny man with his clipboard, Melvin didn't care. They deserved it. He was still struggling to adjust to his death after life! He didn't deserve to be chased by ghostly apparitions.

As Melvin disappeared out of the library and into the corridor outside he failed to notice the soul of the miscellaneous behind him. It wasn't interested in the flamingo-legged idiot or the tiny man. It wanted Melvin Richardson. It recognised him from before and wanted its revenge.

# Souled As Non-Refundable

M elvin reached the end of the corridor. He felt out of breath but knew he couldn't be. He was dead. He wasn't in his body; he was the glue (he refused to think of himself as poo as had been described to him by his so-called lawyer) that held the body and soul together. And poo... I mean glue... didn't breathe. But Melvin certainly felt out of breath right now which was a shame because the ghoulish creature was right behind him; and it wasn't out of breath!

Melvin screamed and fell backwards. The entity hovered above, about to strike at any moment. His eyes clamped shut. He felt the creature inches from his face which made his cheeks turn to ice. Terror shot through his body. The creature was touching him; death was caressing his face.

It stopped. Melvin was motionless, screaming silently inside. Had it gone? He needed to see. Slowly opening his eyes, he saw the tennis-ball pupils glaring at him. He saw the needle teeth ready to bite. The creature screamed in his face and Melvin could do nothing but turn away from the horror above him.

A doorway close by. Could he reach it?

As Melvin tried to crawl from under the ghoulish entity it quickly grabbed him by the tighter than tight swimming trunks and began pulling him down the corridor. Melvin flipped onto his side, his hand squealing across the wooden flooring. He pushed himself towards the door handle to grab it as he passed, his fingers just reaching it in time. The handle turned, allowing the door to swing outward.

Melvin remained clung to the door handle as the ghoulish

creature pulled on his swimming trunks.

The strength of the entity was great, pulling his trunks down to his ankles.

The elastic in them was greater, wrapping around his feet.

Melvin was now in mid-air, hands on the door handle and feet holding his swimming trunks as the apparition pulled on them. He was glad he had paid that little bit extra for a quality pair!

After unsuccessfully trying to pull Melvin down the corridor and only managing to successfully pull down his knickers, the creature released him in rage. Melvin fell to the floor in a heap. The creature circled the air above him.

Melvin stood and tried to run through the newly-open door to escape the ghoulish creature, forgetting his swimming trunks were around his ankles. He fell forwards and crashed into the room followed closely by the raging soul of the miscellaneous.

The double doors of the Grand Soul Library slowly opened. Mr Fitzwilliam peered around the doorway, followed by the tiny man beneath him. The coast seemingly clear, the pair walked cautiously into the corridor.

"We'll have to get the cleaner to put the Miscellaneous back in the briefcase," Mr Fitzwilliam almost whispered, "and sling it out of the chute."

"Probably too late for Mr Richardson." The tiny man wondered what horrors Melvin would be enduring right now.

"He's only poo," Mr Fitzwilliam's eyes were dashing all around, ready to leg-it if the miscellaneous soul appeared again, "he only asks pointless questions anyway. He's trying to spoil the plan."

"Yes," the tiny man frowned, "the plan?"

"I've told you," Mr Fitzwilliam spoke as they began walking

down the corridor, "forget the odd catch. Wherever Mr Richardson's soul was going before we caught it in our net must be where all the souls go! Imagine it; a place where all the souls in the back pocket of the universe go. We'll be rich!"

"That's if they go somewhere." The tiny man wasn't convinced.

"Of course they go somewhere!" Mr Fitzwilliam declared. "Everything goes somewhere!"

The tiny man still wasn't convinced.

"Don't worry," Mr Fitzwilliam appeased his diminutive friend, "I'm just trying to make us some money so we can re-tyre."

"Yeah," the tiny man agreed, "the ones we got are a bit bald."

Suddenly a scream sounded from around the corner. It stopped the pair in their tracks. The tiny man tried to hide behind his clipboard as Mr Fitzwilliam froze beside him.

Just then, a hairy creature on a unicycle with a three-foot-wide moustache rolled around the corner with a bag on its back. The creature looked a little bit like a monkey with its longer shaped head and arms to its knees as it peddled by.

"It's okay," Mr Fitzwilliam sighed his relief, "it's just the pre-man!"

"Post!" The moustached creature spoke like an upper-class aristocrat as it threw a sealed envelope towards Mr Fitzwilliam and continued to cycle onwards, hitting its head on every light fitting as it rolled away.

"He needs a bell on that bike!" The flamingo-legged man spoke as he began opening the envelope to read the letter inside.

"At least he's not swinging from the lights again!" The tiny man pointed out.

As the pair continued to walk down the next corridor the tiny man noticed the red-coloured letter the flamingo-legged man was reading.

"Everything okay?" The tiny man asked. He knew it wasn't. Red-coloured letters were either notices that your life mortgage was expiring or letters from the taxman. Bad news either way!

Yellow-coloured letters were from some other company that Grand Old Designs Ltd had passed your details onto in order to sell you something, and green-coloured letters had been sent to you by mistake. But red-coloured letters… you might as well move to the Urinals of Uranus if you received one of those!

"All fine." Mr Fitzwilliam lied after he had read it, pocketing the letter in his jacket.

"If your mortgage term is ending…"

"It's nothing like that," Mr Fitzwilliam knew the tiny man had seen the colour of his letter, "it's the people of Pluto's Posterior."

The tiny man frowned. He knew they were nice people. Why would they be sending red-coloured letters?

"They noticed one of the souls was missing from the last delivery." Mr Fitzwilliam clarified.

The tiny man knew of the mistake. Melvin Richardson's soul had meant to be in the batch of ten they had sent to Pluto's Posterior but it had fallen out of the package which meant they had only sent them nine souls, one short of the pre-paid consignment.

"That's no worry," the tiny man still didn't understand the panic on Mr Fitzwilliam's face, "just refund them for the missing soul."

"We sell them as non-refundable," Mr Fitzwilliam tried to smile, "and as far as they're concerned we owe them a soul."

"How about one of the miscellaneous souls?" The tiny man offered. "We don't have to sling them all into space. We could dress one up a bit. Make a fake ID."

"They aren't going to fall for that," Mr Fitzwilliam snorted, "they're the rejected souls they sent us back! That's why we sling them into space and blow them up. Besides, everyone has those new-fangled scanners these days! They'd see through the deception."

"They're the people of Pluto's Posterior," the tiny man was sure that they were so passive they wouldn't send anyone a red-coloured letter, "they'll wait till we catch another. We'll send them eleven in the next batch."

"They won't wait," Mr Fitzwilliam replied softly, "they've already sent our details to the debt collectors. That's who sent us the letter!"

The tiny man went pale. He knew the debt collectors that operated in the back pocket of the universe. They were the Marzipans (the people of Mars 2, not the almond-based confectionary product). And the Marzipans were mad (bonkers, not angry).

"I knew releasing Mr Richardson's soul was a mistake," the tiny man couldn't contain his fear, "we should've just sent it to Pluto's Posterior! We could've always caught another one in order to let it go and follow it!"

"It'll be fine," Mr Fitzwilliam was ever the optimist, "when Mr Richardson's soul gets to wherever it's going, we'll be able to pay them the missing soul and a lot more besides!"

The tiny man didn't reply. He had stopped walking and was glaring inside an open door. "I don't know about Mr Richardson's soul, but his poo's gone into the Fast-Forward Room."

Mr Fitzwilliam followed the tiny man's eyeline and stared inside the room. Within it, on the back wall, a clock's fingers were whizzing around at an incredible speed. In the centre of the room a splodge of pink goo was stuck to the floor, eyes within it blinking rapidly.

The so-called lawyer knew what he was staring at. The pink goo was Melvin Richardson.

# The Fast-Forward Room

**M**elvin had to escape the ghoulish creature and had tried to run towards the room with the open door to find a hiding place. Forgetting that his ankles were tangled within his swimming trunks, he had fallen headlong through the doorway and onto the cold floor in the empty room.

He screamed and covered his head, face down on the wooden floor. The apparition was just behind him and Melvin expected it to be on top of him. But it wasn't. All was quiet.

He slowly uncovered his head and looked up. A clock on the back wall ticked merrily away, keeping perfect time. Melvin frowned. Five-and-twenty past three. What time zone was this?

Melvin rolled onto his back, fear screaming within. He gasped as he saw the ghoulish creature in the doorway, covering his face with his hand. Peeking through his fingers, he saw the creature wasn't attacking him. It was silent and still.

The ticking of the clock continued.

Melvin sat up with his hands by his sides. The creature was at the other side of the doorframe, seemingly frozen. It had its arms up by its head and its eyes and teeth were protruding from its face. But the creature remained motionless; fixed in position at the entrance to the room.

Melvin stood, immediately untangling and pulling up his swimming trunks. He walked slowly towards the doorway, in-specting the entity for any sign of movement. He could see none. He looked around the doorframe. The door opened outward and so Melvin couldn't slam it closed in the creature's face. But then,

Melvin couldn't get through the doorway either. The ghoulish apparition ensured the way out to the corridor was blocked.

Melvin looked around. He wasn't sure why the apparition wasn't flying into the room to try and kill him but right now he didn't care. Could he even be killed? He was already dead; his body was under the Mediterranean Sea on Earth and his soul on its way to Heaven. Well, maybe Heaven. Could be Devon for all he knew! Somewhere, anyway.

But could Melvin Richardson, as he was now, be killed? If anything could do it, it was the creature before him. Yet it was unmoving; for now.

Melvin looked around for another way out. Another door or hidden passageway. There was none. The only way in or out was the doorway which was blocked by the ghoulish creature.

Besides a metal desk and chair in the corner of the room the huge clock and a thermostat by the door were the only other things in the room. Melvin was dead. He didn't feel the warmth or cold and so had no use for a thermostat. And he no longer had a use for timekeeping.

Twenty-seven minutes past three, according to the huge clock. It was ticking by at the same rate as the clocks on Earth. But from which time zone?

Melvin checked the doorway once more. The ghoulish creature still hadn't moved. Had it given up? Could it somehow not enter this room?

Sighing heavily (sighing what, he didn't know – he didn't breathe), Melvin picked up the metal chair and placed it in the centre of the room. He sat and faced the entity which was still frozen in the doorway.

"Okay," Melvin began, "I seem to be stuck in here for a while.

Until you move, anyway. So, tell me, who are you?"

There was no answer from the frozen creature.

It was half-past twelve, according to the huge clock. Melvin jolted himself awake. He was still sat on the metal chair and he wiped the drool from his chin as his senses returned. Had the creature by the door moved? Was it closer to the room?

Melvin stood and put the chair back under the table before inspecting the ghoulish creature. It was a ritual he had gone through for as long as he could remember. He knew the apparition's features like the back of his hand and could tell the slightest movement. It hadn't happened at once. It wasn't half-past twelve later in the day. It was half-past twelve later in some other day. Melvin had lost count.

Each day was the same. He would sit. He would talk to the creature. He would check it closely for any sign of movement. Recently he had started to fall asleep due to tiredness. He hadn't felt tired since his death but spending day after day in a room with only the statue of a ghost for company had taken its toll on Melvin. He had even started to drool.

But today, whichever day that was, he had noticed that the ghoulish creature had moved. He could see slightly more of the needle teeth than before. Was this new or had the apparition been moving all along and Melvin had only just noticed? Was it just moving very, very, very slowly?

He held up his hand to touch the creature's face but stopped himself. He had stopped himself every time. One day he would have the courage to touch the creature, maybe even push it out of the way, but not today. Today he sat in the centre of the room, without the chair, and continued his one-sided conversation.

Nineteen minutes past one. The ticking of the clock kept constant as it ticked away the days, or was it years? More sleep. More drool. The tiredness increased.

One minute to twelve. Some other day. Some other time. Melvin couldn't sit up anymore. He was so tired he had lay on his back at quarter to nine one day and stared at the ceiling till one minute to twelve this day. Time meant nothing anymore. The clock on the wall was the countdown to his eternal rest. His doomsday clock. It always felt like he would sleep forever with the very next tick.

Suddenly Melvin heard a sound. It was the first sound he had heard since he could remember. The first sound that wasn't his own voice since he had entered his tomb. It was a scream. A wail of horror. It brought back long-lost memories. A time so distant he couldn't quite visualise it.

The sound echoed throughout the room. Melvin blinked.

"Hello." He managed to summon the strength to speak. He didn't know how. He couldn't feel his mouth move.

Then he saw it above him. The creature. It was in the room and moving around as freely as Melvin had once done. Melvin wasn't afraid anymore. In fact, he wasn't sure what he was!

The creature looked down at him as if curious. Did it not recognise him?

It came closer with teeth outstretched. Its eyes were bulging.

"Hello." Melvin repeated.

The creature recognised the voice and suddenly screamed at him. Placing its hands upon Melvin, it was ready to strike.

Mr Fitzwilliam and the tiny man stared into the Fast-Forward

Room as the fingers of the clock on the back wall flew around at great speed. The pink goo in the centre of the room was still.

"He's in the Fast-Forward Room!" The tiny man declared once again.

Mr Fitzwilliam blew air from his mouth. "I better get in there before he expires." He placed his briefcase on the ground. "Get the shovel."

"You could always leave him in there," the tiny man posed, "after all, you expire in there, you expire out here."

"People have gone in those places to die," Mr Fitzwilliam's voice had sadness within it, "it's not fair on the rest of us out here."

The tiny man didn't question the flamingo-legged man's remark and ran to the store room, returning with the required implement.

Mr Fitzwilliam grabbed the shovel and took a deep breath as he stared inside. If it had been his choice he wouldn't have allowed the builders to put a Fast-Forward Room on his transport. But he had forgotten to tell them not to. These types of room were as common as the kitchen or back passage; everyone had one! All they were to Mr Fitzwilliam was a death trap.

Holding his breath, Mr Fitzwilliam stepped inside. The speeding clock on the back wall instantly slowed to normal speed. It read two minutes past two. He looked back beyond the doorframe to the corridor outside. The tiny man was frozen still, holding an unmoving clipboard. Mr Fitzwilliam knew he wasn't frozen, of course, he was just moving very, very, very slowly.

"Mr Richardson," the flamingo-legged man walked to the gunge on the floor, "you've seen better days. Good job there are no mirrors in here."

A pair of eyes appeared in the goo, followed by a mouth. "I'm so tired."

"You've been in here a while," Mr Fitzwilliam replied, "why didn't you leave?"

Suddenly a ghostly-white face appeared in the goo. It wasn't Melvin's; it was the soul of the miscellaneous.

Mr Fitzwilliam jumped backwards.

"It's okay," the mouth of Melvin spoke wearily, "I seem to know all about her now. She's a mathematician, you know! She won't harm you."

"You must have mixed." Mr Fitzwilliam replied.

"What does that mean?" Melvin hadn't spoken aloud for so long and was finding it tiring.

"Let's get you out of here before you expire." Mr Fitzwilliam had no time to explain and scraped the shovel along the floor underneath the pink goo.

The creature within the goo snarled as Mr Fitzwilliam picked up the thick substance with the shovel. Melvin's eyes blinked rapidly. The ghoulish creature tried to lift its head, unsuccessfully.

Mr Fitzwilliam hoisted the pair through the air and out into the corridor. As the substance passed the threshold of the doorway it instantly changed back into Melvin and the creature before they had entered the room. The creature flew into the air, free from the goo it had been trapped inside, and Melvin fell to the wooden floor, his swimming trunks around his ankles once more.

"Looks tiny." The ghoulish creature snarled from above, now able to communicate with Melvin.

Melvin frowned at the remark and pulled up his trunks before realising the creature meant the size of the tiny man beside him.

Melvin looked back inside the weird room he had been entombed inside for so long. The fingers on the clock on the back wall were spinning around at high speed. That wasn't right, surely?

In the doorway, Melvin saw a rapidly aging man with flamingo legs stood with a shovel in his hands.

# The Radio Room

An elderly Mr Fitzwilliam stepped into the corridor and instantly became his younger self. His dizziness was replaced with fear when he noticed the ghoulish creature floating in the air above Melvin.

He jolted on his flamingo legs at the sight. But the creature didn't attack. As Melvin stood to his feet the entity flew behind him as if it was the one that was scared of the others.

"We seem to know each other now," Melvin gave a smile as if to signify he didn't want to know the ghoulish creature now, "so, how about that!"

"Well," Mr Fitzwilliam gained control of his fear, "you've spent a long time together."

"What is that place?" Melvin was still tired from the amount of time he had spent in the odd room. He felt like a 1000-year-old who was about to have another birthday!

"The Fast-Forward Room," Mr Fitzwilliam slammed the door to the room closed, "it's not a place you want to be."

"The clock on the wall," Melvin noted, "out here it's flying by! Inside the room it's normal."

"Depends on your point of view." Mr Fitzwilliam handed the shovel to the tiny man, who ran away to put it back in the store room.

"You were growing old really quickly in there," Melvin snapped, "and out here you're back to normal!"

"So are you," Mr Fitzwilliam pointed out, "it's why the door opens into the corridor; wouldn't take long for the wood to rot if it opened inwards!"

Melvin frowned, trying to grasp what the so-called lawyer was talking about. "You mean everything goes faster in that room?"

"Do you think it's called the Fast-Forward Room for a laugh?" Mr Fitzwilliam remarked.

"Well, the big clock in there doesn't seem to be rotting away." Melvin felt embarrassed at his stupidity, which said a lot considering the idiots he was surrounded by.

"Well, the clock's not made of wood." Mr Fitzwilliam replied.

"What's it made of?" Melvin was still struggling to keep up.

"A substance so non-perishable it's thought to last longer than it would for the old fashioned dial-up internet to download Gone with the Wind, the extended director's cut version, complete with an interview with Clarke Gable and out-takes from the film!"

Melvin was quiet for a moment, half-struggling to work out how long that would take and half-struggling to work out if the so-called lawyer was lying to him again. He wished he had another half to think clearly. "So, what's the non-perishable substance?" He finally stopped trying to work it out.

"Old men's nostril hairs."

Melvin blinked rapidly.

"They don't have an expiry date!" Mr Fitzwilliam declared.

"I'm sure they do." Melvin was still blinking.

"And when you leave the room," Mr Fitzwilliam explained, "you reset to the moment before you went in but you keep all the memories of the time you spent inside."

"I know," Melvin remembered his time inside the weird room, "I got tired! I thought I was already dead and didn't need to eat or sleep; why would I get tired?"

"I've told you," the flamingo-legged man didn't understand why it was so hard to comprehend, "you are the poo that holds your body and soul together. What do you think happens to poo after a long time?"

"I don't really think about it after its flushed away." Melvin wasn't sure what he was supposed to think.

"Out of sight, out of mind." Mr Fitzwilliam shook his head. "Poo turns into goo. Your consciousness fades away; a sensation you experience as tiredness. Takes a long time, of course," the flamingo-legged man picked up his briefcase. "but nothing lasts forever, Mr Richardson, unless you're made from nose hairs! The Fast-Forward Room just gets you to the end quicker."

"How quicker?" Melvin barked. "How long did I spend in there?"

"Point of view, Mr Richardson," Mr Fitzwilliam smiled and began walking down the corridor, "we all have an expiry date. That's why you shouldn't go in that room. You die in there and you die out here."

"How long have I got until I turn into that gunge?" Melvin chased after the so-called lawyer, followed by the now-friendly ghoulish creature.

Mr Fitzwilliam ignored his question, mainly because he didn't know.

"Look," Melvin yelled with more purpose, "I need to get my life back! My body is under the Mediterranean Sea and I don't want to turn into that goo!"

"Okay, Mr Richardson," Mr Fitzwilliam stopped walking and glared at Melvin, "if you want your body to be moved from under the sea on Earth, I think Beryl's your boy." He nodded to another room behind Melvin.

Melvin looked behind him at a sign above a door that read 'Radio Room'.

"Go in there," Mr Fitzwilliam snapped, "Beryl will be able to help."

Before Melvin could reply, Mr Fitzwilliam was walking briskly away.

"And what are you doing?" Melvin called after him.

"You want your soul back, don't you?" Mr Fitzwilliam disappeared around the next corner.

"You were going to blow it up earlier!" Melvin yelled down the empty corridor, remembering the bomb in the briefcase.

He did want his soul back, but wasn't convinced the so-called lawyer would help him with that. However, first thing's first, he thought, maybe Beryl in the Radio Room could help him move his body from under the waves on Earth. Taking a deep breath (I know), Melvin entered the Radio Room.

Dials, knobs and switches surrounded him. The room was filled with old fashioned looking equipment and a small woman sat in a leather chair with huge earphones on her head; Melvin assumed this was Beryl. She was listening to some kind of whistling noise and occasionally adjusting the dials in front of her to make sense of it. She immediately stopped when Melvin and the miscellaneous soul entered the room.

"It's okay," Melvin noticed her fright at the sight of the creature behind him, "this is a friend."

"It's a Miscellaneous." She gasped, removing her headphones.

Melvin glanced behind him at the floating entity, which seemed hurt by the remark. "Why are they called the Miscellaneous?"

"Because they can't be alphabetised." She replied like the answer was something everyone knew.

Melvin still didn't understand. "Why not?"

Beryl relaxed in her chair, breathing out her momentary fear.

The man before her really didn't know anything!

"Because we don't know their names." She grabbed a pipe and a lighter from the counter beside her and burned the tobacco within it into life. It calmed her nerves after sudden shocks and seeing a floating Miscellaneous was certainly a shock.

Melvin remembered the Grand Soul Library and the soulcases lettered A-Z with the souls placed in their corresponding case depending on their surnames.

"But she has a name," Melvin knew all about the creature behind him as his consciousness had combined with it whilst trapped in the Fast-Forward Room for however long, "she's called Sharon Taylor!"

"Ahh," the woman relaxed even more, "then she's a T-soul."

Melvin glanced behind him again, noticing the entity was trying to smile.

"And who are you?" The woman enquired through fresh smoke rings.

"I'm Melvin Richardson."

"Then you're an R…"

"I'm not a soul." Melvin interrupted.

"Oh," the woman looked disgusted and reached for her spray, "then you're poo!"

She sprayed the air in-between herself and Melvin. The floating soul sneezed and growled at her. It hated being cleaned.

"I've been sent in here so you can help move my body on Earth," Melvin stepped forward into the haze of spray, "the flamingo-legged man sent me in here."

"Benny sent you in?" She smiled and glanced at a photograph on her desk, replacing the spray and taking another suck on her pipe.

Melvin followed her eyeline and looked at the picture on her desk. It was a framed pair of flamingo legs with the top part of the body cut off. Was that a picture of Mr Fitzwilliam's legs? Why would she have a picture of his legs?

Beneath the picture, Melvin saw some kind of delivery sticker usually seen on parcels for posting. An address had already been filled in; 'Grand Old Designs, Front Porch, 214 Front Porch, Front Porchville, please go to the back porch.' Melvin frowned at the first line of the address.

"Grand Old Designs." He spoke aloud.

"It's where I live," Beryl blew another smoke ring, "Front Porch on the planet GOD. My grandad left me that in case I want to visit one day."

"Grand Old Designs is a planet?"

"You have to put the planet name first because you don't want to end up on the Urinals of Uranus by mistake!"

Melvin remembered the description of Grand Old Designs that the so-called lawyer had given him and it had seemed more like some big corporation. It also seemed like a big fat lie but that was beside the point right now. It was actually a planet?

"It's everything," Beryl spoke as if she had read his thoughts, "the planet, the transport; if you go to the toilet what comes out is theirs."

Melvin scrunched up his face and stepped back.

"Anyway," she smiled through another smoke ring, "I can't help you."

Melvin took a moment to remember what he had asked for; moving his body on Earth, that was it! "Benny seemed to think you could." He could tell she liked him. Maybe if she knew it was the so-called lawyer's idea she would help him more readily.

"I listen to the radio waves given off by the planets we pass," Beryl explained, "and put together the recordings so people can watch their lives back when they die. I don't move bodies."

"So, you put together that story of my life?" Melvin remembered the farce that was the video clip of his life story.

"That's me." she took another puff of her pipe.

"I was told it was put together by guardian angels." Melvin winced at the lies he had been told by the so-called lawyer. "You're not very accurate, are you?" Melvin didn't want to offend her.

"I'm the most accurate audio and visual expert onboard," she was offended, "I take radio waves from televisions, microwaves, phones and computers to get the best all-round picture of a person's life! I put together the story of Jesus from the radiation that came from his beard!"

"*The* Jesus?" Melvin struggled to believe what he was hearing.

"That's right," Beryl stuck out her chest as she sat proud, "*the* Jesus Winterbottom of 714 Cranley Street." Another smoke ring of confidence bellowed from her lips.

Melvin grimaced; not *the* Jesus, then.

"Well, I'm not sure why Benny thinks I can help you move your body on Earth," she placed the pipe on the counter and picked up her huge headphones, "sorry."

"Maybe," Melvin ushered her not to place her headphones back on, "he thought that someone as smart as you would find a way."

She smiled, placing the headphones back on the counter. "He said that?"

Melvin and the soul of Sharon Taylor smiled, although the floating soul's needle teeth looked more horrifying than comforting.

"The only thing I can do is see if there's been any reports of your missing body," she turned to her apparatus and started twisting dials, "by hacking into the local area's audio and digital signals. Maybe I can create some feedback to get in touch with them."

Melvin's smile widened. Finally, it seemed like he was getting somewhere. He had hope at last. She knew what she was doing!

"Where is your body?"

"The Mediterranean Sea," Melvin replied quickly, "off the coast of Benidorm."

"Is that Spain?"

Melvin nodded slowly as his hope quickly died.

Beryl placed her headphones on and began twiddling hastily. Melvin and the soul of Sharon Taylor remained silent.

"We seem to be too far away to create feedback," she spoke slightly louder from under the headphones, "so, I won't be able to contact them. But I think I found something from a Spanish television news channel."

She flicked a switch which made a voice echo through the speakers in the room:

"Unt, err, manos... was washed-eos... err, up on the beach-eos; this morning... eos."

"Isn't the word beach 'la playa' in Spanish?" Melvin was confused.

"It's the translator." Beryl switched off the broadcast and smiled at Melvin. "I'll listen to it through the headphones without it. You probably don't speak Spanish."

"Neither does your translator." Melvin wasn't amused.

Beryl placed the headphones on and listened intently. "They found a body washed ashore..." she looked back at Melvin.

"Is it mine?" Melvin's hopes were alive again. "They found my body? It's out of the water?"

"I think so," she strained her ears, "it's been identified by a fellow holiday maker."

Melvin almost clapped. He had been on a lads' holiday and one of them must have identified his washed-up body.

"I wonder if they've told my folks at home." Melvin's mood sank as the thought struck him.

"I'll check the telephone calls for the area." Beryl fiddled with more dials.

"You can get it that quick?" Melvin was impressed.

"They're not really radio waves anymore," she replied, "since we went digital we can pull things through faster. It's a bugger of a monthly payment though!"

Melvin was nervous as Beryl switched the next recording through the main speakers again.

"I know, it is a shame…"

The voice was male, too crackly for Melvin to recognise. Must be one of the lads on holiday with him, he figured, talking on a mobile phone.

"…his parents are devasted. They don't want anything lavish though. It'll cost enough to get the body home when the Spaniards have finished with it. Just gonna be a simple cremation with a few close mates…"

The crackling overtook the voice and Beryl flicked off the sound. That's all there was.

Melvin was pale, his mind focusing upon what he had heard.

"You okay?" Beryl asked the shaking man.

Melvin didn't reply. He dashed out of the Radio Room and down the corridor to try and find the so-called lawyer, the miscellaneous soul of Sharon Taylor remaining close behind him.

"I need my soul back now!" Melvin yelled at the top of his voice. "My body! They're going to cremate my body!"

# Spacial Delivery

**M**elvin was about to give up his search for the so-called lawyer in the maze of corridors when he heard a familiar voice call for him. It was the tiny man with his huge clipboard, ushering him to follow. It wasn't long before Melvin and the soul of Sharon Taylor were in a room with a giant pane of glass in place of one of the walls. Beyond the glass was darkness.

"Did you find what you were looking for, Mr Richardson?" Mr Fitzwilliam was in the room, looking into the darkness beyond the glass. His briefcase was on the floor by his side.

"What is this place?" Melvin stepped further into the room.

"This is where it all happens!" Mr Fitzwilliam spun around to face Melvin and opened his arms. "This is the Driving Room."

Melvin looked around the room. It was empty. Completely empty. No controls. No dials. No switches. No steering wheel. What exactly *happens* in here?

"Takes a moment to digest, doesn't it?" The tiny man stood beside Melvin and beamed with pride as he looked around the room. "The technology in here is astounding. There's no finer room onboard."

Melvin was hastily looking around for something to look at but there was nothing.

Suddenly he heard a sneeze from behind him and he spun around. In a dark corner of the room was a small figure. Not as small as the tiny man but still small. He hadn't noticed it before due to the darkness.

As his eyes adjusted, Melvin found himself looking at a mole-like creature staring at the wall. On its face were a pair of spectacles halfway down its nose.

"That's Brian," Mr Fitzwilliam declared, "the driver!"

"Is that a mole?" Melvin squinted harder at the figure.

"He's the best driver in the back pocket of the universe," the tiny man boasted for him, "and we got him for a foot of soul!"

"A soul's foot." Mr Fitzwilliam corrected.

"Aren't moles blind?" Melvin ignored the remarks, more concerned at having a blind mole at the helm.

"Nonsense!" Mr Fitzwilliam barked. "He has perfect hearing!"

Melvin frowned deeply, assuming the so-called lawyer had misheard him.

"He can't see anything," Melvin glanced back at the mole, "he's facing the wall for a start!"

"What do you want to see?" The tiny man was confused.

"If I was the driver I'd want to see where I was going!" Melvin was bewildered.

Mr Fitzwilliam walked to Melvin and placed his arm around his shoulder before walking him to the huge pane of glass.

"Look out there," the flamingo-legged man began, "what do you see?"

Melvin strained his eyes into what he assumed was outer space. "Nothing."

"Well," Mr Fitzwilliam turned to face Melvin, "you're as bad as Brian then!"

Melvin struggled to phrase his reply but couldn't. He didn't think they would listen anyway. Turning to the centre of the room, the tiny man had joined them by the window along with the floating soul of Sharon Taylor.

"I need my soul back." Melvin decided to get the conversation onto more pressing matters.

Another sneeze from the mole in the corner.

"We're following it now." Mr Fitzwilliam replied with a beaming smile.

Melvin looked at Brian, the so-called driver who was facing the wall, and turned to look at the blackness outside before turning to the pair of idiots once more. "Are you sure we're following it now?"

"Where else would we be going?" The tiny man enquired.

"I have as much interest in following your soul as you do, Mr Richardson." Mr Fitzwilliam tapped his shoulder.

"I'm not interested in your interests." Melvin shrugged the so-called lawyer's hand away.

"Sounds like a bank." The tiny man interjected.

"I don't want to follow it," Melvin went on, "I want to catch it."

"Ohhhh," the tiny man shook his head, "we can't catch it."

"It's going way too fast!" Mr Fitzwilliam declared.

"Then get Brian to speed up!" Melvin began to panic. He needed his soul, and quickly, before his body on Earth was stuffed into an incinerator!

"We can't speed up." Mr Fitzwilliam replied.

"Not with these bald tyres." The tiny man's head was still shaking.

"Bald tyres?" Melvin was close to exploding. "We're in space, what do bald tyres matter?!"

"They slow us down, of course!" Mr Fitzwilliam declared.

"But," Melvin glanced between the so-called lawyer and the tiny man, wondering which one was the thickest, "there's nothing in space!"

The pair mumbled something between themselves as if to not believe what they had heard.

"Well," the tiny man seemed confused, "we are in space. That's something."

"He's right, you know." Mr Fitzwilliam backed up his diminutive friend.

"No," Melvin couldn't believe they didn't understand the concept, "I mean there's no friction."

"Of course not!" Mr Fitzwilliam barked. "No one argues with space!"

"It's a vacuum!" Melvin didn't know how many different ways he could explain it.

"Does he mean the space vacuum?" The tiny man asked his flamingo-legged friend.

"It's next to the ironing board, isn't it?" Mr Fitzwilliam replied.

"Space *is* a vacuum!" Melvin spoke slower. "It means there's nothing in it."

Mr Fitzwilliam could hardly contain a smile. No wonder the people of Earth hadn't passed their Basic Living exam!

"No, no," it was the flamingo-legged man's turn to explain things in a slower way, "the space between your ears *is* a vacuum. Space *has* a vacuum. The Sucker-3000; best vacuum cleaner in the back pocket of the universe! They switch it on every bi-annual-semi-tri-monthly quarter to keep things clean."

Melvin blinked rapidly. "Switched on by who?"

"By whom." Mr Fitzwilliam corrected.

Melvin continued to blink.

"Keeps the dust from settling on planets." The tiny man added.

Suddenly the idiocy was interrupted by a loud scream in the

doorway. It was enough to make even the soul of Sharon Taylor jump!

Melvin spun around to see what looked like a monkey riding a unicycle with a three-foot-wide moustache. It had a bag over its shoulder and was carrying a huge parcel which it threw to the floor by Melvin's feet.

"Thank you, pre-man!" Mr Fitzwilliam waved as the monkey wheeled back out into the corridor, banging its head on the light fittings as it rolled away.

"Who was that?" Melvin didn't quite catch what the so-called lawyer had called it.

"The pre-man." The tiny man replied.

"Deals with the post." Mr Fitzwilliam explained.

"Then don't you mean postman?" Melvin frowned.

"Why would we mean that?" Mr Fitzwilliam didn't understand.

"You're the post-man." The tiny man pointed out.

"I work in IT." Melvin replied.

"Worked." Mr Fitzwilliam corrected. "Then you died."

"So, you're the post-man." The tiny man repeated.

"That's the pre-man." Mr Fitzwilliam stepped forward to inspect the parcel.

"Deals with the post." The tiny man concluded.

Melvin could have screamed at the nonsense he was being bombarded with, but he didn't get the chance. At that moment the parcel by his feet burst open and two shadowy figures stood tall from within it. They had what looked like guns and immediately called for silence, even though the room was silent.

They were the Marzipans.

"Benny Fitzwilliam," one of them growled, "we're here to collect payment of one Earth soul on behalf of the people of Pluto's Posterior."

The soul of Sharon Taylor cowered behind Melvin.

The other shadowy figure pointed its gun at the floating soul and fired what looked like a red laser. It was scanning it. "That soul is a reject," it flicked the laser off and holstered the gun, "do you have a viable Earth soul?"

"She's not a reject!" Melvin defended his new friend before realising that was probably a stupid thing to do.

"It has no identity document," the shadow gnarled its reply, "therefore, it is a reject. We have a spare bomb if you want to get rid of it?"

Melvin kept his mouth shut.

"I have a soul for you." Mr Fitzwilliam smiled at the two shadowy figures. The smile was through fear. These were the Marzipans; the maddest bunch of creatures in the back pocket of the universe!

"Bring it." The shadow's voice rasped.

"It's not on me," Mr Fitzwilliam patted down his jacket as if to prove what he had said, "it's out there." He glanced through the huge window and into outer space.

"Now wait a minute," Melvin knew the so-called lawyer was talking about his soul and wasn't going to stand for it, "that's my soul you're talking about, isn't it! Well, I need it back. So, I'm afraid you'll have to find another!"

The shadowy figure still holding its gun stepped up to Melvin and placed the barrel under his chin.

"Well, I'm not using it anyway," Melvin whimpered in fear, "it's all yours. Maybe I can get you my mother's as well."

"You will take us to the Earth soul," the shadowy figure with the holstered gun growled at Benny Fitzwilliam, "then your debt is repaid."

"No problem." Mr Fitzwilliam smiled.

The Marzipan with the gun under Melvin's chin stepped back.

Melvin blew out his fear in an exasperated spell of air. "It's a good job I'm made of poo."

"You will come to our vessel," one of the Marzipans growled at Mr Fitzwilliam, "it is faster than this pile of poo."

"Excuse me?" Melvin took offence.

"It means the transport." Mr Fitzwilliam spoke through the side of his mouth.

"Oh," Melvin realised, "carry on."

"No problem." Mr Fitzwilliam picked up his briefcase. "Can't forget my banana and crisps."

"You too!" The shadow growled at Melvin.

"But, I…" Before Melvin could finish his sentence the shadowy figure placed a red sticker on his forehead and he disappeared into thin air along with the soul of Sharon Taylor who was right on Melvin's shoulders.

Mr Fitzwilliam and one of the Marzipans were the next to vanish, leaving the tiny man in the Driving Room with only one of the shadowy figures.

"You will leave." The Marzipan barked at the tiny man. It had a job to do whilst it was onboard and didn't want anyone in its way.

The tiny man didn't need telling twice and ran off into the corridor wondering what he was going to do now!

The shadowy figure looked around. The room was empty. It smiled and walked to the parcel box from where it had arrived. Picking out a pair of flamingo trousers, the Marzipan put them over its legs with a smile.

It stopped suddenly. Someone had sneezed.

The shadow squinted into the corner of the room and saw a mole facing the wall. Frowning, it returned its attention to the parcel. There was one more item it needed.

Snarling with a grin, the Marzipan picked up a bomb from the parcel. It was time to take care of Benny Fitzwilliam's transport like they took care of rejected souls.

# Knees Are The Knockers To The Soul

**M**elvin appeared in a small room surrounded by various pieces of paper, boxes and pigeon-holes. He heard a snarl behind him and realised that the soul of Sharon Taylor had been transported along with him. But transported to where?

Suddenly the so-called lawyer appeared with one of the shadowy figures.

"Where are we?" Melvin spoke up immediately.

"In the Marzipan's post room, it would seem," Mr Fitzwilliam explained as he ripped off the red sticker on his forehead, "on their vessel. The stickers are used for returning parcels. Although most people just post letters, not themselves." He glared at the shadowy figure.

Melvin ripped off the red sticker from his own forehead, choosing not to ask any questions. The answer would probably be a riddle in any case.

"It's the quickest way to collect." the Marzipan growled.

"Well, you are the debt collectors." Mr Fitzwilliam rummaged through a pile of stickers on the counter by his side. "You must have every delivery address in the back pocket of the universe, with pre-paid returns here. You even have my transport address." He picked up a couple of stickers and turned to the shadowy figure.

"Put them back!" The Marzipan growled.

Mr Fitzwilliam turned back to the counter. "I guess you got permission from Grand Old Designs Ltd to use all these."

"Come," the shadowy figure snarled, ignoring the idiot, "you will take us to the Earth soul."

Melvin, the soul of Sharon Taylor right behind him, and Mr Fitzwilliam, complete with briefcase in hand, were marched through dark corridors at gunpoint by the shadowy figure until they reached a room entitled 'Cockpit'.

"I dread to think what's in there." Melvin's voice trembled.

"It's their driving room." Mr Fitzwilliam frowned at him.

"Oh."

The inside was cramped. Melvin wedged himself into a seat at the back and allowed the soul of Sharon Taylor to float beside him. There was another shadowy figure sat in the seat by the front window surrounded by dials, knobs and switches. He even had a steering wheel! Not like the nonsense he had seen on the so-called lawyer's ship. Or transport. Or whatever he called it.

"Which way?" The Marzipan in the driving seat gnarled.

Mr Fitzwilliam struggled into the seat beside him as the shadowy figure with the gun remained stood by the doorway.

"Well," Mr Fitzwilliam began, "it's kind of... that way." He pointed straight forward.

"Co-ordinates?" The driver growled.

"North?" Mr Fitzwilliam spoke like he wasn't sure himself.

Melvin frowned. He was sure there wasn't a North in space but he had also been sure there wasn't a vacuum cleaner either until he had been argued into thinking it by the so-called lawyer.

"He doesn't know where it is!" The Marzipan with the gun growled in anger. "But we have the soul's poo." It turned the gun towards Melvin. "Stick your finger in there!" It pushed the gun forward.

Melvin glared down the barrel, fear exploding within.

"Do it!" The shadowy figure pushed the gun forward once more.

Melvin slowly raised his hand to the barrel of the gun. His eyes darted from the shadowy figure to the gun barrel. Terror coursing through his veins, he slotted his index finger into the barrel of the gun.

"What are you doing?" The Marzipan was filled with confusion.

Melvin couldn't reply as his fear crippled him. Even the soul of Sharon Taylor took a gulp of fright.

"I said stick your finger in there!" The Marzipan nodded its head beyond Melvin.

Melvin turned his head to see an open slot on the counter beside him which read 'place finger here' flashing a bright red colour, and realised the shadowy figure had previously tried pointing to it with the gun. Coming to his senses, Melvin took his finger from the barrel and placed it in the open slot on the counter.

There was a beeping sound which made Melvin pull his hand back.

"I have a lock." The driver growled, turning the wheel.

"It'll take some doing to catch a soul!" Mr Fitzwilliam remarked smugly. "You'll need to break the Soul Barrier, and for that you'll need a Soul Drive. And I'm afraid that's completely impossible!"

"Is it?" The shadow in the driver's seat gnarled.

"Yep," Mr Fitzwilliam was sure, "because I've just made it up!"

Suddenly a computerised voice came through some speakers; "Soul Drive initiated."

"Oh." Mr Fitzwilliam watched the darkness of space outside turn white as the vessel broke the Soul Barrier.

"Follow me!" The shadowy figure with the gun ordered Mr Fitzwilliam and Melvin to follow.

They slowly rose to their feet and were led through more dark corridors to a pair of step ladders leading to a hatch in the roof.

"Here," the Marzipan ordered them to stop, "when we are upon the soul you will catch it."

Mr Fitzwilliam looked at his briefcase and back at the shadow. "I can't do that."

"Is it capable of transporting souls?" The shadowy figure growled.

"Oh, yes," Mr Fitzwilliam replied, "the briefcase isn't the problem. The problem is I'll die if I go into space. You see, I'm not the one who's dead."

Both Mr Fitzwilliam and the Marzipan glared at Melvin.

"Wait a minute," Melvin held up his hands and backed into the soul of Sharon Taylor, "I don't even know what's going on!"

"The vessel is going to fly underneath your soul," Mr Fitzwilliam explained, "while you go up there, through that hatch, and catch it in here!" He held up the briefcase.

"Through that hatch is space?" Melvin looked up.

"You're already dead," Mr Fitzwilliam pointed out, "you can survive space. It's not a problem for you."

"I'm not going out there!" Melvin declared.

"Then how are you going to get your life back?" Mr Fitzwilliam smiled. "You need all three states to live. You're just the poo and eventually you'll turn into that pink goo you love so much. Your body on Earth is going to be cremated. The only way you can begin to save yourself is to get out there and get your soul."

Melvin was silent for a moment. The so-called lawyer was right, but there was still something off about the whole thing.

"You only want my soul to pay off your debts." Melvin glared at the flamingo-legged man, trying to see any sign that he could trust him.

Mr Fitzwilliam leaned towards Melvin. "Let me worry about that." He lifted up the briefcase for Melvin to take and gave his widest smile.

Melvin glanced at the shadowy figure holding a gun at them, and back to the so-called lawyer. What other choice did he have? None he could think of, and grabbed the briefcase, turning to the Marzipan. "What do I do?"

The instructions given had been clear enough. The air in the corridor had been sucked out so that the hatch could be opened when the vessel was directly underneath the soul. Mr Fitzwilliam and the shadowy figure were in another corridor separated by a door with a small window in it. Once the vessel had caught up to the soul a signal would be given to Melvin through the small window so that the hatch could be opened and Melvin's soul could be scooped into the briefcase. What could go wrong?

The soul of Sharon Taylor floated alongside Melvin, as did the now useless pair of step ladders. Briefcase in hand, Melvin awaited the signal to go through the hatch above him. Panic was building inside him. He didn't want to venture out into space. What if the so-called lawyer was wrong? What if it would kill him?

Suddenly Melvin felt something roll inside the briefcase. He remembered the other briefcase that had been in the Grand Soul Library with the bomb in it. Had Mr Fitzwilliam swapped them in an attempt to double-cross the Marzipans?

Smiling uncontrollably, Melvin flicked open the briefcase to have a look inside.

No, he hadn't swapped the briefcase at all! It was the banana that Melvin had felt, falling from one side of the briefcase to the other. Of course, Mr Fitzwilliam hadn't swapped briefcases; he wasn't that smart!

Melvin glared through the small window where the so-called lawyer and the Marzipan were, his hopes sinking once more.

"Are we close yet?" Mr Fitzwilliam, in an adjacent corridor, was panicked. If this went wrong the Marzipans would surely kill him.

"Not yet." The shadowy figure replied with a growl, fiddling with a monitor on the wall. "I don't want the alarm to go off when the hatch is opened."

"Why not?" Mr Fitzwilliam asked with a tremble in his voice.

"We only have one alarm," the shadowy figure replied, "the driver won't know if it's the hatch that's been opened, if we're under attack or if someone's not refilled the toilet roll holders properly!"

Mr Fitzwilliam left him to it, fidgeting like mad. He hated being this close to a Marzipan and turned to look through the small window at the floating Melvin. He caught the floating man's gaze, giving him a nervous thumbs-up as if to convey that all would be okay.

Unfortunately, Melvin took the thumbs-up to be the signal that meant it was time to open the hatch and retrieve his soul.

The step ladders now halfway down the corridor, Melvin used the soul of Sharon Taylor to push himself upwards towards the hatch. He failed to see Mr Fitzwilliam behind him through the small window waving his arms for him to stop after realising his mistake. It was no use. Melvin had opened the hatch. The alarm sounded throughout the Marzipan vessel.

Melvin didn't hear it as he floated outside into a brilliant white. He smiled as he swam deeper into the whiteness, the briefcase at the ready. This couldn't be space, Melvin thought. This had substance.

There were eyes all around him. The brilliant white was like the thick gunge in the sceptic tank onboard Mr Fitzwilliam's transport. The thick gunge he would eventually turn into! But this wasn't made from poo; this was all soul.

The eyes around him narrowed. Hissing noises rang in his ears. The souls were rejecting him.

Suddenly, through the brilliant white sea, something emerged. Something that was drawn to him. Closer. The feeling of familiarity filled Melvin. He smiled at the sight. It was his soul.

A hand emerged from the whiteness and grabbed Melvin's. They had found each other; the poo and the soul, together again, in some weird dreamy yoghurt-commercial style of scene. Melvin even thought he could hear a choir lingering on a high-pitched note somewhere.

Suddenly another hand grabbed Melvin's soul and tried to pull it away. The singing had stopped. It was a choir, and Melvin's soul was a chorister now. The other members refused to let their contralto-voice go!

Melvin pulled back, swotting the other creatures with the briefcase. It was no use. The chorus of souls began singing again! All around Melvin. All with varying tones. It was the perfect opposite to a night-terror; like ice cream on steroids! And it was horrible!

As his soul was about to turn and sing the chorus of Kumbaya,

My Lord with the rest of them, another soul came flying on scene; the soul of Sharon Taylor. It grabbed Melvin's soul and pulled it from the others, bundling it inside the briefcase. The soul of Sharon Taylor then grabbed Melvin by the swimming trunks and pulled him back through the hatch into the Marzipan's vessel once more.

In another part of space entirely, the tiny man was running around Benny Fitzwilliam's transport with no idea what he was going to do! Passing the Radio Room, he stopped and went straight inside without knocking.

Beryl was sat smoking her pipe and clutching the framed picture of the flamingo legs. She jumped to her feet and replaced the picture when she saw the tiny man.

"Can I help you?" She snapped.

"Benny's been taken by the Marzipans," the tiny man with his huge clipboard replied in haste, "and there's one loose onboard somewhere! I need you to find it!"

"Oh my!" She took the pipe from her mouth in shock.

"I'll go back to the Driving Room and see if I can get Brian to get us to safety." The tiny man spoke quickly.

"Okay." Beryl replied, still sunned.

"Don't go to the Marzipan if you find it," the tiny man warned, "just tell me where it is."

"How did they get here so fast?" Confusion overtook Beryl. "I didn't hear any ships nearby."

"Spacial Delivery." The tiny man replied.

Beryl turned to look at her own Spacial Delivery sticker by the photo of flamingo legs. She could just use it to despatch herself home right now. Leave the transport until the Marzipan had gone.

She stopped herself from that line of thought immediately.

Benny Fitzwilliam was in trouble. Well, they were all in trouble, but especially Benny. She had to stay and help.

As the tiny man left the Radio Room she began fiddling with the dials on her desk. She would listen to every room on the transport until she found the one with the Marzipan in it. It would be easy enough to do. The Marzipans had a distinctive breathing noise like an asthmatic chain-smoker having sex on a Bouncy Castle.

The first twenty-three rooms were no good, Beryl heard nothing that would make her think the Marzipan was in any of them. It was the twenty-fourth room that Beryl knew she had hit the jackpot; the coarse breaths were unmistakable. Checking the room that she was listening into, a frown took over her face. It was the Toilet Room. She hoped she was listening to the Marzipan and not something more sinister. There was only one way to find out and Beryl headed off to check it out against the tiny man's warning.

Through quiet, winding corridors Beryl tiptoed to the toilet door. She would find out what the Marzipan was up to. She would do it for Benny!

Inside the Toilet Room, beside the huge bowl in its centre, the shadowy figure with flamingo-legged trousers held the bomb tightly. Its disguise was perfect. Any onlookers would see the flamingo legs and think it was Benny Fitzwilliam. Legs were how everyone recognised everyone else. They were the distinguishing feature that made individual recognition not just easy, but possible.

As the old saying goes, knees are the knockers to the soul.

The Marzipan stood silently by the bowl, awaiting further instructions. If things didn't go according to plan with retrieving the viable soul it was on standby to initiate 'plan-b' (b for bomb in case you missed it).

Beryl was by the Toilet Room door, looking on in fear. She didn't see a Marzipan awaiting instructions. With the fabulous flamingo-legged disguise, Beryl only saw Benny Fitzwilliam stood by the toilet bowl with a bomb in his hands. Her eyes glistened as the moment struck her; Benny was in league with the Marzipans!

# Double Cross

"**G**ive me the briefcase!" The shadowy figure pointed the gun at Melvin in the corridor which had been filled back up with air (the corridor not the gun). The alarm had been cancelled. On the plus side the toilet roll holders were now all full.

"I need it," Melvin held the briefcase tightly, "to get my life back!" He glanced towards Mr Fitzwilliam, who was stood beside the Marzipan. "You said you'd help me."

Mr Fitzwilliam remained sheepishly silent.

"Is this all you're about?" Melvin blasted him. "Money?"

"You don't know what that soul is worth," the shadowy figure growled angrily, "now, hand it over and we'll be on our way."

"Do something." Melvin pleaded with the so-called lawyer.

"Get me that briefcase," the Marzipan turned to the flamingo-legged man, "and your debt is paid."

Mr Fitzwilliam took a deep breath and walked slowly towards Melvin. The soul of Sharon Taylor hissed as he came near.

"I told you before," Mr Fitzwilliam spoke softly, "everyone has an expiry date." He placed a hand on Melvin's backside.

Melvin frowned deeply and pushed it away.

"It's where the expiry date is," Mr Fitzwilliam was sombre, "no one checks back there."

Melvin took a moment to process. "Why are you telling me about my expiry date now?"

"You never know when you might need to check it." Mr Fitzwilliam replied.

Melvin frowned. Did the so-called lawyer not know how to give a straight answer without shrouding it in nonsense?

"The briefcase!" The Marzipan interrupted the two idiots with a wave of its gun.

Mr Fitzwilliam placed his hand on the briefcase and pulled it towards himself. Melvin wouldn't let go. The soul of Sharon Taylor hissed once again.

The shadowy figure coughed, making the point that the gun was aimed squarely at Melvin. It was over, Melvin realised. He had lost. With one last glance at the briefcase Melvin let it go along with any chance he had of getting his life back.

Mr Fitzwilliam smiled and walked back to the Marzipan, handing over the briefcase. "My debt is settled."

"I'll check the contents first." The shadowy entity growled, placing the briefcase on the floor.

"Naturally." Mr Fitzwilliam knew it would.

The shadowy figure opened the case to the white light of the soul inside. Aiming the gun at it, a red laser fired for a second. It was scanning it.

"That's a cool gadget you got there," Mr Fitzwilliam remarked, "a pistol and a scanner all in one! Does it turn the lights off as well?"

The shadowy figure looked up at Mr Fitzwilliam. "If you're trying to distract me," it slammed the briefcase closed with the soul inside, "it won't work."

Mr Fitzwilliam smiled in reply.

The scanner beeped. The soul in the briefcase belonged to Melvin Richardson. It was viable. Mr Fitzwilliam's debt had been repaid.

"Do I get a receipt?" Mr Fitzwilliam enquired innocently.

The shadowy figure stood and took out a receipt pad and a pen. He scribbled down the contents of the briefcase and signed his name with one cross. Mr Fitzwilliam smiled as he pocketed his proof of payment.

The shadowy figure picked up the briefcase, aiming the gun at Melvin once more.

"And what am I to do with you?" The Marzipan growled.

"Send him back to the transport with me," Mr Fitzwilliam offered, "he's no use to you. He's not worth anything. He's poo. He'll bring the value of the soul down if nothing else!"

Melvin scowled at the double-crossing so-called lawyer in silence. He felt sick. He knew he shouldn't have trusted him. All the so-called lawyer had done since his untimely death was lie to him.

"I have a better idea," the shadowy figure snarled, "he wants a life. I'll give him a life." Laughter emerged from the Marzipan.

"I can't see how you're going to do that," Mr Fitzwilliam frowned, "he didn't have a life when he was alive!"

The shadowy figure ignored the flamingo-legged idiot and stepped towards Melvin. "You want a life?"

Melvin remained frozen with fear. The soul of Sharon Taylor was also afraid and held onto Melvin's shoulders.

"You Earth people need three states to live," the Marzipan continued, "the body, the soul, and the poo. You already have two."

"But you have my soul." Melvin glanced at the briefcase in the shadowy figure's hand, his voice trembling in fear.

"It means the Miscellaneous behind you." Mr Fitzwilliam reluctantly explained.

"But…" Melvin was struggling to keep up, "that's not my soul."

"I can send you back to Earth," the growl of the Marzipan deepened, "with the reject behind you!"

"You can send me to my body?" Melvin had a moment of hope.

"It won't be your body." The shadowy figure laughed.

Melvin shot a glance to the so-called lawyer for clarification.

"It will be the miscellaneous soul's body, but with you inside it." Mr Fitzwilliam's throat was dry.

"You're only the poo that holds them together!" The shadowy figure snarled.

"Don't worry. It can't do it!" Mr Fitzwilliam declared. "The only way it could is..."

"You mean I'll become Sharon Taylor?!" Melvin interrupted in anger.

"...if you give it the soul's identity!" Mr Fitzwilliam finished his sentence in dismay.

The Marzipan's laughter grew. Taking out a delivery sticker it handed it to the flamingo-legged man. It needed the idiot to write the destination address of where it was about to send Melvin Richardson and the miscellaneous soul.

"I can't," Mr Fitzwilliam shook his head, "I've done enough already."

The shadow raised its gun and handed Mr Fitzwilliam a pen.

Reluctantly, the so-called lawyer wrote 'Earth, Sharon Taylor's body' on the delivery slip and signed it with two crosses before handing it back to the Marzipan. He knew the address he had written was enough. The miscellaneous soul would automatically seek out its own body from there and Melvin Richardson would be the glue that held them together.

"Wait," Melvin began, "you're going to send me back to Earth with Sharon Taylor's soul so I'll end up in her body?!"

The shadowy figure slapped the sticker on Melvin's forehead and pressed upon it. Before Melvin had a chance to say anything else both he and the soul of Sharon Taylor disappeared in an instant.

"Well, Mr Fitzwilliam," the Marzipan holstered its gun and held out a hand for a shake, "that shut him up. Our business is concluded."

Mr Fitzwilliam shook the Marzipan's hand. "What's to stop him using the return slip?"

The shadowy figure held up the return portion of the sticker that he had ripped free so that Melvin had no chance to use it to return. "His trip is one way only."

The Marzipan burst out laughing, which prompted Mr Fitzwilliam to join in.

The shadowy figure then handed Mr Fitzwilliam another delivery slip, this one pre-written with Benny Fitzwilliam's transport details upon it. Again, the return portion had been ripped free so he couldn't return.

"We'll let Pluto's Posterior know your debt has been settled in full." The Marzipan tapped the briefcase with a smile. "Don't accrue debts in future, Mr Fitzwilliam. We won't be as pleasant next time."

Mr Fitzwilliam forced a smile before sticking the delivery sticker to himself and pressing on it to activate the despatching mechanism.

He was back on his transport in an instant, appearing in the Post Room. The pre-man almost fell off his unicycle in shock.

Apologising profusely, Mr Fitzwilliam ran across his transport to the Driving Room where the tiny man was pleased to see him. Brian was indifferent; he didn't see him arrive.

"They let you go!" The tiny man declared. "It went well then?"

Mr Fitzwilliam ripped off his delivery sticker and threw it to the ground. "There was a slight hitch," he explained, "I lost Mr Richardson."

"It went well then." The tiny man smiled.

Onboard the Marzipan vessel, the shadowy figure was also smiling as it held the briefcase in its hands. It enjoyed its work, collecting the debts of idiots across the back pocket of the universe. No one got away without paying; the Marzipans prided themselves upon that!

The shadowy figure took out the gun, which was also a long-distance radio device (and yes, it turns off the lights as well), and contacted the Marzipan that was still onboard Benny Fitzwilliam's transport.

"No need for the bomb," the shadowy figure spoke into its gun as it placed the briefcase on the floor to inspect its prize once more, "it all went according to plan."

"Okay." The voice crackled in reply.

"I have the viable soul." the shadow unclasped the locks of the briefcase, "and now we'll sell it back to Pluto's Posterior for three times what it's worth!" It growled with laughter as it opened the briefcase wide and glared inside.

The laughter stopped. Anger took over in an instant and the Marzipan let out a scream into the air.

"Bennnnyyyyyyyyyyyyyyyy Ffffffffffffffffffffffff..."

The briefcase was empty, except for a packet of crisps and a banana.

# Hastings And Blow

"Benny Fitzwilliam!" His father shouted from the doorway. It was time for supper and the boy had been out all day.

The supper table was full, as always, with everyone from the street. They all paid the entrance fee, of course. Benny's father, Johnny Fitzwilliam, insisted upon that!

It was always a race to finish supper for Benny, but his father wasn't at the table for some reason. Most unusual, indeed.

"Where's father?" Benny asked the maid.

Suddenly a stranger sat beside Benny burst into laughter. Somewhat rude, Benny thought, until the stranger stood and unzipped the kangaroo legs he had on to reveal a pair of flamingo legs. It had been his father sat beside him all along!

"How's Small School?" Johnny Fitzwilliam asked his son at bed time.

"We've just started learning Cosmic Geography." Benny beamed.

"Well, don't forget," Johnny Fitzwilliam replied sternly, "you don't need Big School."

"That's where you learn what happens after you die," Benny was interested in that stuff, "and why we're here."

"The real world is where the money is." His father smiled.

"Don't you want to know why we have two souls?" Benny asked.

"Because we have two feet." His father replied simply, taking out a folded-up piece of paper. "I want you to keep hold of this."

"What is it?" Little Benny was intrigued.

"A copy of instructions on how to build something," his father handed his son the paper, "you won't find that in Big School. You must keep it safe, Benny, just in case."

Benny took the paper with a curious frown, not understanding what his father was on about. He unfolded it to reveal a list of instructions on how to build a Fast-Forward Barn. "What's that?"

"I'll show you." His father replied with a smile.

Little Benny and his father were outside by the barn. His father smiled at him before flinging open the door. It looked normal to little Benny, who still didn't understand what the fuss was about.

His father told him to stay put for a moment whilst he brought a cow over to the barn. As he ushered it inside, Benny laughed as the cow suddenly began to run around inside at an incredible speed.

Backwards and forwards it went like Superman overdosing on Smarties. Every movement at hightened speed, little Benny was now realising why his father had called it the Fast-Forward Barn.

The boy's laughter soon stopped as he noticed the cow was suddenly on its side and getting thinner. It didn't take long for little Benny to realise what was happening; the cow was dead and decomposing at an accelerated rate!

Little Benny turned away in disgust. His father closed the door and turned to him.

"It's the Fast-Forward Barn," his father explained, "speeds everything up that goes inside."

"What's the point of it?" Little Benny looked at his father. All he saw was a room that brought death quicker for whoever was inside it.

"If I could tweak the speed of it," his father went on, "imagine the crops we could grow. What would take months for everyone else would take us minutes. We'll be rich, but you mustn't tell anyone. This is between you and me, Benny boy."

"You and I." Little Benny corrected.

"It's serious, Benny," his father spoke sternly, "no one is to know. Not even the maid."

"So, if she asks why you took me to the barn after bed time, I've to say it's between you and me?"

"Okay," his father thought about it for a second, "you can tell the maid. But no one else! If my boss gets wind of this it won't be ours anymore."

Little Benny giggled uncontrollably.

"You're laughing at the 'gets wind' bit, aren't you?"

Little Benny nodded.

"Look," his father was upon his flamingo knee, grabbing the boy's hand with the folded-up piece of paper within it, "remember what I told you."

"Don't go upstairs when you're up there with the maid." Little Benny replied.

His father blinked rapidly. "No, not that." He took the paper from the boy and stuffed it inside his son's pyjama pocket. "Keep that safe! If anything happens to me the Fast-Forward Barn is yours."

Johnny Fitzwilliam was early at work the next morning. Hastings and Blow was a small team, consisting of Asherah Hastings, Barry Blow and Johnny Fitzwilliam. They had started their star-cleaning firm some twenty years ago and were originally Fitzwilliam, Hastings and Blow until their first job had cost them their savings.

It was Johnny Fitzwilliam's fault. He had come up with the

idea of the star-cleaning firm and advertised accordingly. He had turned up to their first job with a bucket and sponge ready to clean Mr Swank Castle's star cluster. Unfortunately, the ladders he had brought hadn't been long enough to reach them. I mean, seriously, what kind of ladder would reach the stars anyway?

Mr Swank Castle sued them. Mr Johnny Fitzwilliam paid the price.

He had to sell his Sunday-best soul and forfeit his name on the business, which was therein known as Hastings and Blow. They weren't star cleaners anymore, but now specialised in reorganising constellations with the use of newly-invented transports. Johnny Fitzwilliam was no longer a partner. In fact, he had only been kept on through sympathy as his name was a laughing stock across the back pocket of the universe thanks to the high profile Swank v Fitzwilliam court case. It had spawned a number one spoof hit called 'Ladders to the Stars', and Betty Paige had even starred in a comedy satirising the incident called 'My Husband's Tiny Ladders'. If anyone asked, Johnny Fitzwilliam didn't work for Hastings and Blow.

"You've messed up again, Johnny," Asherah Hastings wasted no time in getting to her point, "Mr Slax wanted a Bear Constellation."

"I followed the drawings," Johnny Fitzwilliam glanced at Barry Blow, the draughtsman of the group, "it's not my fault they weren't right!"

"My drawings are perfect!" Barry Blow defended himself, standing squarely at Asherah's side.

"What's this?" Asherah Hastings held up the drawing made by Barry Blow.

Johnny Fitzwilliam had no choice but to tell the truth. "A bear."

"And what's this?" She held up a photograph of Johnny Fitzwilliam's work.

The flamingo-legged man glared at the photograph of the stars he had arranged for Mr Slax. "A penguin?" He wasn't sure himself.

"A penguin," Asherah repeated, "and not a very good penguin! You wouldn't see Betty Paige trying to save that, would you?"

Johnny Fitzwilliam shrugged in agreement. The successful actress, and famous animal lover, Betty Paige certainly wouldn't help whatever animal that was supposed to be!

"I've been distracted with…"

"You get distracted a lot," Asherah snapped, "like your first job with Frozen Dairies."

"I bought that ice-cream van with my own money!" Johnny Fitzwilliam defended himself.

"And parked it on Mercury!" Asherah replied in disbelief.

"I didn't know what would happen," Johnny Fitzwilliam remembered disappointing the children on his rounds the next day, "anyway, I didn't know you needed references. I set up this business!"

"Your name hasn't been on the business for sixty years." Asherah pointed out.

"We've been thinking of changing things for a while now, anyway." Barry Blow spoke softly as if to soothe the moment. It didn't work.

"It's nothing that Johnny Fitzwilliam needs to know." Asherah Hastings held up a hand to silence Barry, before sitting behind her huge desk.

"I set up this business," Johnny Fitzwilliam repeated himself, "I put everything into it!"

"I'm sorry," Asherah Hastings wasn't sorry, "you're fired."

It was no use trying to argue, Johnny Fitzwilliam was jobless.

He had no Sunday-best soul to sell for money and had no back-up savings to rely on. He didn't even have a van anymore, the previous one having melted alongside his 99s due to the searing heat of the planet Mercury. Johnny Fitzwilliam was worthless and his status would only drag his family down too.

He was quiet at supper time that night. And later, when little Benny was in bed, Johnny Fitzwilliam made his way to the barn. It was time to do the universe a favour. Maybe it would help his family, at least.

Unlocking the barn door, Johnny Fitzwilliam strolled inside. It felt the same as being outside, but he knew it wasn't. If only he had more time to develop the Fast-Forward Barn. To make it how he had envisaged. But it was no use. Hopefully his son would re-create the barn from the instructions he had given him. Hopefully his son would make something of his life.

As he sat on the damp floor, the wooden boards had long since rotted away, he looked through the open door and into the outside world as a thought struck him. He *did* have more time to work on his Fast-Forward Barn! Time outside was passing at a very, very, very slow rate. In the barn, it was flying by. Point of view, Johnny Fitzwilliam realised. He had all the time in the world in here to make the necessary tweaks required and hardly any time at all would have passed out there!

As he left the barn with new-found purpose a strange feeling hit him. The feeling of success at last, Johnny Fitzwilliam figured.

His tweaks took time but that didn't matter to Johnny Fitzwilliam. It was all point of view! He learned he could slow the rate at which time passed within the barn, and kept it at the same speed as the outside world whilst he brought in some plant seeds and water. He would plant them, flick the speed up to 'plus 64' and stand outside for 30 seconds whilst they grew at an incredible speed. A perfect plan; what could go wrong?

The maid. That's what.

The maid had noticed the barn door was open that morning. She assumed that Johnny Fitzwilliam was at work, because why wouldn't he be? And locked the barn door without checking inside.

At the same moment the lock had clicked Johnny Fitzwilliam had ramped up the speed inside the Fast-Forward Barn. Unfortunately, he had twisted the dial beyond breaking point and, you guessed it, broke the dial.

He turned to the locked door and ran to it, trying to get out. He couldn't. The barn had initially been built by Hardman and Sons and they prided themselves on their strong timbers. And so, Johnny Fitzwilliam was trapped inside his Fast-Forward Barn, unable to slow the rate at which time was passing. From his point of view time was ticking by at the normal rate. But to the outside world he would be dead in minutes.

Supper time again. Little Benny looked around for his father but with no success. Was he in disguise again?

It was bedtime and little Benny voiced his concerns to the maid who was tucking him in. Her reply was to smile and comfort little Benny with platitudes. Little Benny wasn't comforted.

When the maid had left, little Benny turned over and heard a crumpling sound from his tiny flamingo legs. It was a piece of paper in his pyjama bottoms; the paper his father had given him with the instructions on how to build a Fast-Forward Barn. Curiosity overcame the boy and he was in his flipper-slippers heading towards the barn with keys in hand moments later.

What little Benny had seen inside the barn would give the bravest of people nightmares, and he struggled to clear it from his mind as he stood by his father's graveside beside the maid. Bones that turned to dust. The image was seared onto his brain. Curiously, the nose hairs of the skeleton hadn't turned to dust. Little Benny had thought that weird.

Of course, no one believed the boy. When he had scooped up his father's remains and brought them out of the barn something extraordinary had happened. They had instantly turned back into his father's younger self! He was still dead, but at least now he had his flesh back! And the nose hairs, of course.

Asherah Hastings joined the boy at his father's graveside and expressed her sympathies when the funeral service was complete. Little Benny was holding the paper his father had given him in his shaking hands, about to throw it into the ground with his father. He wanted nothing to do with the Fast-Forward Barn. It brought nothing but death.

Turning to thank the grown-up behind him, little Benny recognised her as someone his father had worked with and plunged the folded piece of paper into her hands. Let them have it! Little Benny never wanted to see the Fast-Forward Barn again!

Asherah Hastings frowned as she unfolded the piece of paper the boy had given her. A smile widened across her face as she realised what she was reading; a set of instructions on how to build a Fast-Forward Barn.

She took out a pad of small papers from her pocket and placed the instructions inside for safety. Barry Blow joined her by the graveside as she closed the small book with a smile. The front of the pad was headed with their new business name that Asherah had come up with personally. No longer Hastings and Blow; they were now to be known as Grand Old Designs Ltd.

# Forever Is A Point Of View

Beryl watched who she thought was Benny Fitzwilliam (the flamingo legs, you see) stood by the huge toilet bowl holding a bomb. What was he doing? Had he gone mad?

The Marzipan that was stood by the toilet bowl, wearing flamingo-legged trousers and holding a bomb, was mad. It had heard through its radio/gun/scanner/light switch that Benny Fitzwilliam had double-crossed them and taken the viable soul somehow. So now the instructions were clear; light the bomb and blow Benny Fitzwilliam's transport star high!

The mad Marzipan took out a lighter and lit the fuse of the bomb, throwing it into the toilet bowl (the fire they create on Mars 2 is waterproof, of course). The shadowy figure then took out its return spacial delivery sticker and pressed it to its forehead before disappearing into thin air.

Beryl gasped at what she had seen. Benny Fitzwilliam had thrown a bomb into the toilet bowl. It would end up in the sceptic tank. It would blow the transport star high!

Anger raging through her mind, Beryl ran back towards the Radio Room and her own spacial delivery sticker. She wasn't going to be blown up by the mad Benny Fitzwilliam! It was time for an impromptu visit to her grandad!

Tears flowing down her face as she looked at the photograph of the flamingo legs one last time, she pressed the spacial delivery sticker to her head and disappeared in an instant.

The real Benny Fitzwilliam was at the other end of his transport in the Driving Room with the tiny man, completely unaware that the mad Marzipan had thrown a bomb down the lavatory.

He was thinking back on his earlier deception and smiled at the events that had occurred when he had first appeared on the Marzipan vessel in their postal room;

*"Amazing, you must have every delivery address in the back pocket of the universe pre-paid with returns here. You even have my Transport address." Benny Fitzwilliam picked up a couple of stickers and turned to the shadowy figure.*

*"Put them back!" The Marzipan growled.*

*Mr Fitzwilliam turned back to the counter, **and sneakily pocketed the delivery address labels.***

Mr Fitzwilliam, still thinking of earlier events, turned his mind to the time on the Marzipan vessel as he had handed the briefcase with Melvin Richardson's soul within it to the shadowy figure;

*The shadowy figure opened the case to the white light of the soul inside. Aiming the gun at it, a red laser fired for a second. It was scanning it.*

*"That's a cool gadget you got there," Mr Fitzwilliam remarked, "a pistol and a scanner all in one! Does it turn the lights off as well?"*

*The shadowy figure looked up at Mr Fitzwilliam. **In that instant, Mr Fitzwilliam flicked one of the delivery labels he had screwed up in his pocket into the still-open briefcase.***

*"If you're trying to distract me," it slammed the briefcase closed with the soul inside, "it won't work."*

***But it had worked,** Mr Fitzwilliam smiled...*

The smile was still on Mr Fitzwilliam's face as he walked into the corridor to look inside a small room to his left. He was looking at Melvin Richardson's soul. He knew the Marzipan would open the briefcase to check its contents and had been ready with the spacial delivery sticker. When the briefcase had been closed the soul inside (Melvin's soul) would have squashed against the sticker, activating its despatching mechanism and instantly transporting the soul back to Benny's transport.

The only problem now was Melvin bloody Richardson! Benny hadn't banked on him being sent to Earth inside the body of Sharon Taylor!

Suddenly, a huge explosion broke Mr Fitzwilliam's train of thought. It ripped through the transport knocking everyone that was aboard to the floor.

"What was that?" The tiny man removed the rubble that covered him and picked up his clipboard as he stood on shaking legs.

"It's them." Benny Fitzwilliam was on his back under a pile of debris. Something had exploded onboard and Mr Fitzwilliam knew what that meant; the Marzipans were here!

"It's the sceptic tank that exploded!" the tiny man glared through the huge window before him, watching the remnants of what used to be the tank floating away.

"It's the Marzipans." Benny Fitzwilliam spoke like he was already dead.

"Why aren't they telling us what they want?" The tiny man replied hastily.

"They are," Benny Fitzwilliam breathed his response, "they just don't know that sound doesn't travel through space."

"So, how do we know what they want?" The tiny man helped Benny Fitzwilliam onto his flamingo legs.

"It's why the Marzipans are mad; they never get what they want," Mr Fitzwilliam caught his breath, "because they don't realise that no one can hear them!"

"I think they want us dead." The tiny man was now stood at the window looking into the blackness of space outside.

"It's probably a safe bet." Mr Fitzwilliam replied. He knew what they wanted.

"Well yes, seeing how there's a torpedo heading straight for us." The tiny man pointed his huge clipboard towards the pane of glass beside him.

Mr Fitzwilliam squinted beyond the tiny man. He could see the Marzipan vessel in the cold distance outside and, sure enough, the torpedo it had released that was heading straight for them.

His life crashed before his eyes. Skipping Big School to build his own transport and collect souls for profit, eventually catching Melvin bloody Richardson! It had all led him to this point in time; to the torpedo with his name on it.

But Benny Fitzwilliam wasn't ready to die and made a snap decision to do something about it. In panic, he turned and ran away, the tiny man struggling to keep up.

It was an easy decision to reach in the end, one he remembered his father had taken. If nothing else it would buy him some thinking time.

Time! Mr Fitzwilliam smiled as he sat on the metal chair that wasn't metal in the centre of the Fast-Forward Room. Time was something he had an abundance of now.

He looked beyond the doorframe and into the corridor outside. The frozen image of the tiny man down the hallway holding his clipboard made him smile. The tiny man wasn't frozen, of course, he was just moving very, very, very slowly!

Beside the doorway, a portion of the pre-man's unicycle wheel could also be seen as Mr Fitzwilliam had almost knocked him from it as he ran by him. Mr Fitzwilliam's smile widened at the sight. The monkey-like figure also looked frozen in time, trying to regain balance whilst banging his head on a light fitting above him. He wasn't frozen, of course, he was just moving very, very, very slowly.

Mr Fitzwilliam's smile soon disappeared as he thought of the oncoming torpedo. He knew it would still be heading for his transport, it would just be moving very, very, very slowly like everything else beyond the doorframe.

It seemed fitting somehow. The place he swore never to venture inside again would be his tomb, just like it had been his father's. But what else could he do? Out there was death-by-torpedo in a matter of seconds. In the Fast-Forward Room there were years.

A tear rolled down his cheek as he looked at the seemingly-still tiny man in the corridor. From his point of view he had given the tiny man his own forever to live. Forever, stood in the corridor with his clipboard.

From the tiny man's point of view, however, he would be dead in seconds.

Maybe that's all forever was; a different point of view.

# Epilogue

Far from the oncoming torpedo somewhere in outer space, Earth spun around the Sun as it always did, merrily and with no regrets.

On its surface, the inhabitants wandered around as they always did. Some were partying, a life lived in fast forward. Others were working, a life lived in slow motion. Some were doing nothing in-particular at all! Time for each seemingly going at differing rates depending on the boredom of each individual at any given moment.

One old man was walking through a graveyard with a dozen roses for his wife. His life had been a full one and had seemingly rolled by at great speed. But old age had slowed things down a little, and it was his wife's birthday again.

Roses had been her favourite and even after the ten years since her death he always came by and placed some on her grave on her birthday. He placed them on the gravestone and smiled at the words etched upon it. It was a loving memory. She had been his wife, living at the same speeds he had.

Rest in peace, Sharon Taylor.

Beneath the soil, encased in a wooden coffin, the body of Sharon Taylor lay. But it was far from peaceful. It was inhabited by the consciousness of Melvin Richardson.

He had appeared in the small, dark box having been sent via spacial delivery. It didn't take long for him to figure out where he was and he began kicking and screaming for help.

A coffin! Of course, he was in a bloody coffin! He had been sent into Sharon Taylor's body and God knows how long she'd been dead! What did Melvin expect; her corpse to have been stuffed and placed at the end of some bar? No. She had been buried. And now Melvin Richardson was buried!

Continuing to hammer furiously on the inside of his wooden tomb, he hoped in vain that someone above ground would hear his screams and dig him up.

Above ground there were no screams. Above ground there was only the silence of loving memories.

**TO BE CONTINUED...**

Printed in Great Britain
by Amazon